ROAD TRIP
EXPLORERS

Bath · New York · Cologne · Melbourne · Delhi
Hong Kong · Shenzhen · Singapore

**Ready for a road trip? You can go anywhere—
and see anything—you want.**

**The best roadside attraction:
lemonade!**

Color By Number
Use this guide to complete the picture.
1 - pink 2 - tan 3 - blue
4 - red 5 - orange 6 - yellow

Want to borrow my binoculars?

Let's go rafting down the river.

I can't wait to see the view from the top.

See, the map was right. We're almost there!

Ants love picnics!

We can take a road trip in the sky.

Look who's at the zoo waiting to see you.

Trace over the lines and then make this bird colorful.

There's a lot to see out on the sea.

I'm just nuts about camping.

This jeep can handle a rocky ride.

How about a road trip by submarine?

**There's lots to explore in a toy store.
How many toys do you see?**

You're the captain of the ship.
Where are we headed?

Circle, then color the animals that live in the sea.

Look who's at the construction site.
Can they build you a house
of straw, sticks, or bricks?

It's a traveling library.

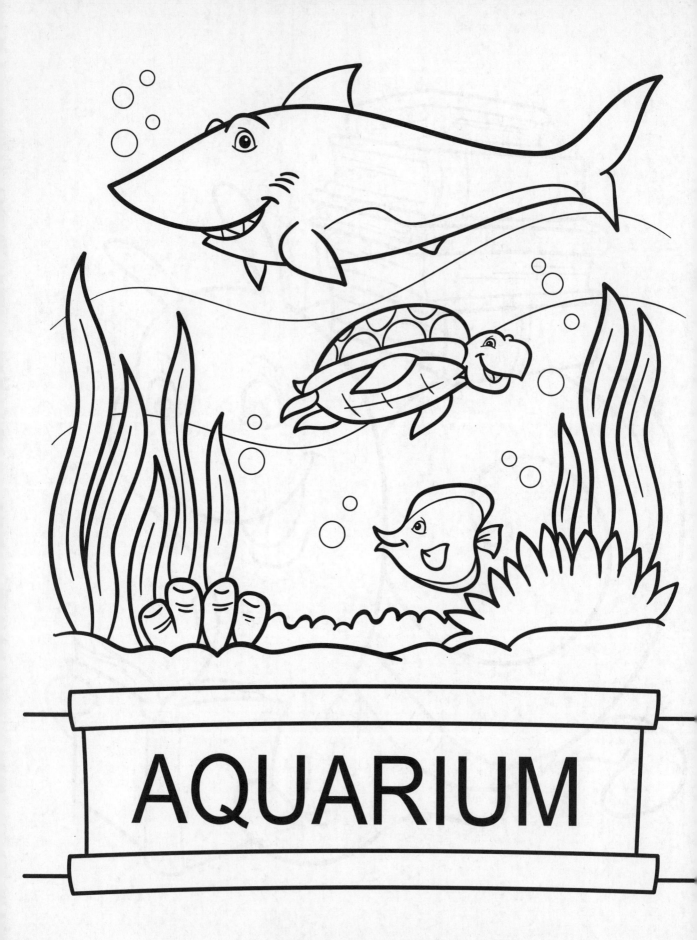

AQUARIUM

Want to dive in to the aquarium?

Look, she's making ice-cube bubbles.
The water must be cold!

Here's a fun way to zip around town.

**This zoo elephant needs you
to trace around the lines.**

**What a bright idea—
a jar of fireflies can light my campsite.**

**When you're done skating in the park,
you and a friend can play some tic-tac-toe!**

Trace this cow.

Greetings from the Moon.

No campout is complete
without roasted marshmallows.

Welcome to Kitty's Bakeshop.

Vroom! Rev your engine and get out on the road.

Color By Number
Use this guide to complete the picture.
1 - yellow   2 - blue   3 - green   4 - brown   5 - purple

It's the best-smelling shop in town.

I spy an adventure.

One picnic, coming right up.

Everything sure looks different
from up here.

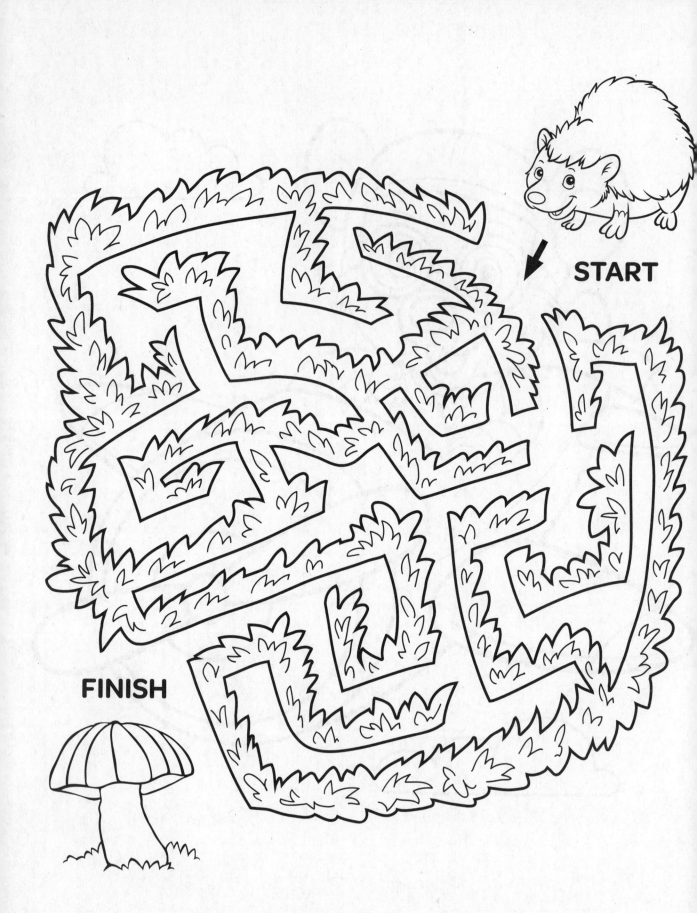

START

FINISH

Which way to the toadstool?

Whooo is in the canoe?

The sweetest stop on any road trip.

START

**Help the bee fly to
the fragrant flower.**

Ah, it's nice to relax outdoors.

I always build a sand castle at the beach,
don't you?

**Connect the dots to see
who is smiling at the aquarium.**

What do you think is happening here?

Going downhill is a breeze.

How tall of a building should I build?

START

FINISH

HONEY

I'm looking for my honey.

**There are no pancakes finer
than the ones at the diner.**

How about these apples?

What a bright and beautiful place!

A puffer fish puffs up when he's scared—connect the dots to see.

A little water and a little love
help garden flowers grow.

**Connect the dots
so the crab can show off
his castle.**

Shall I get you a doggy bag?

1

2

18

17

3

16

15

4

8

11

12

13

14

9

7

10

5

6

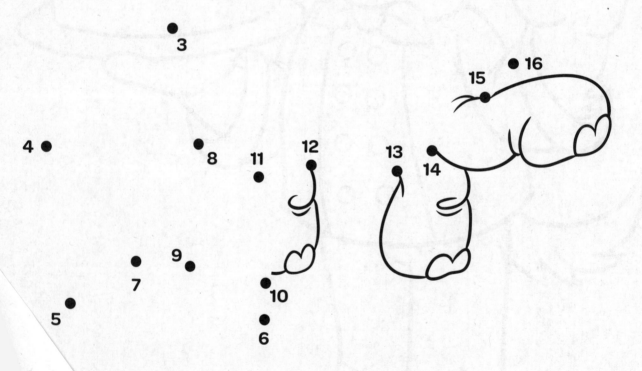

**Connect the dots to finish
this big guy.**

Wow, this plant is taller than me now!

By the side of the road.

This is a great place to explore.

I personally love to travel in the water.

Greetings
from

PLACE
STAMP
HERE

Write a postcard to
someone on Mars.
Draw your favorite
thing on Earth,
address the card,
and even put a
sticker stamp on it.

_____

_____

_____

_____

**What do you think this dino
could see with that long neck?**

Welcome to the farm!

Shhh, Mama is asleep.

Let's drive through the desert.

Color By Number
Use this guide to complete the picture.
1 - pink   2 - brown   3 - green   4 - blue   5 - red

Oh, I love to visit the garden
at snack time.

A

B

C

D

E

F

Circle, then color the things that you would expect to see in a bakery.

Welcome to a bird's version of a car wash.

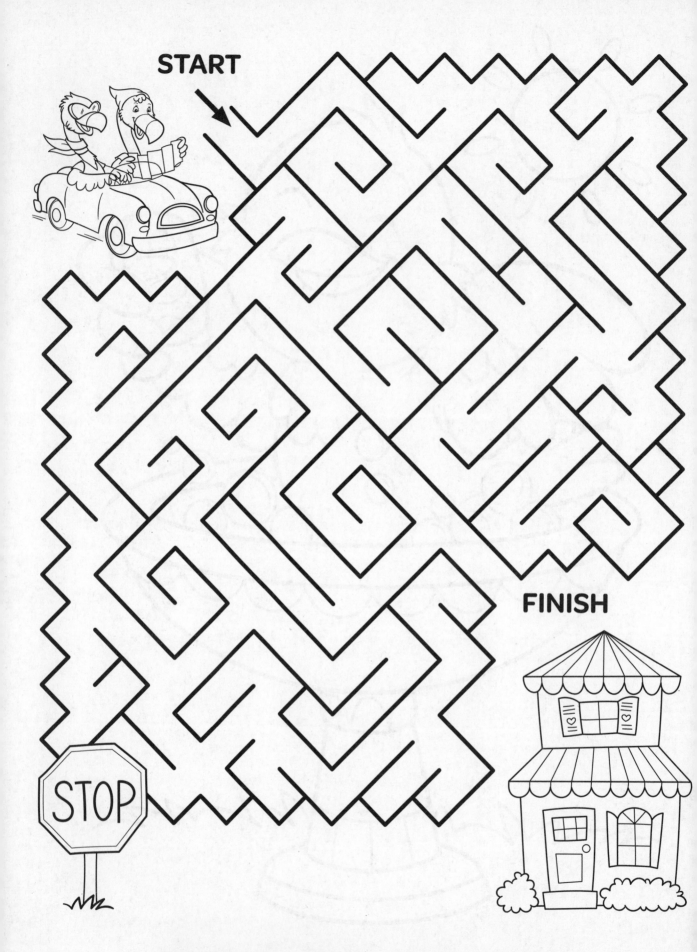

START

FINISH

STOP

Which way to our country house?

Special delivery, winging its way to you!

Would you like to stop at this sweet shop?

Will you join me for lunch on the farm?

Trace the lines around this crabby guy.

Where should we swim to today?

I'm jumping for joy at seeing you.

You and a friend can play some out-of-this-world tic-tac-toe.

A

B

C

E

F

D

G

Circle, then color the things you would see at the airport.

No job is too "ruff" for a firefighter like me.

Yum! Corn!

Draw a pattern on this dinosaur.

If you pay the fare, I'll take you anywhere.

**After a day playing in the snow,
this is a warm and cozy place to go.**

Trace the horse so she can prance.

Pretty flowers by the side of the road.

A

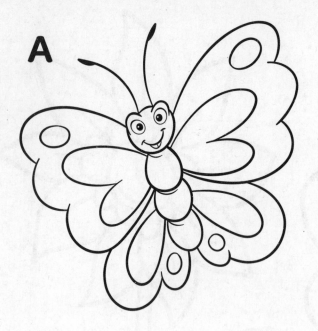

B

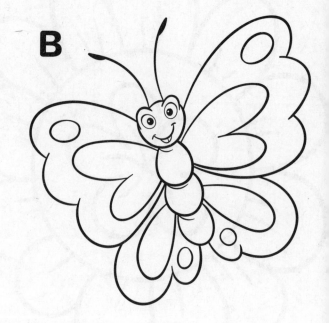

C

D

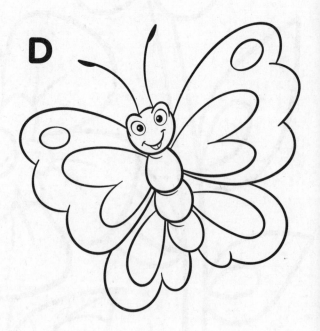

Your answer:

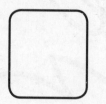

Which butterfly is different from the rest?

I'm a cowboy riding my horse!

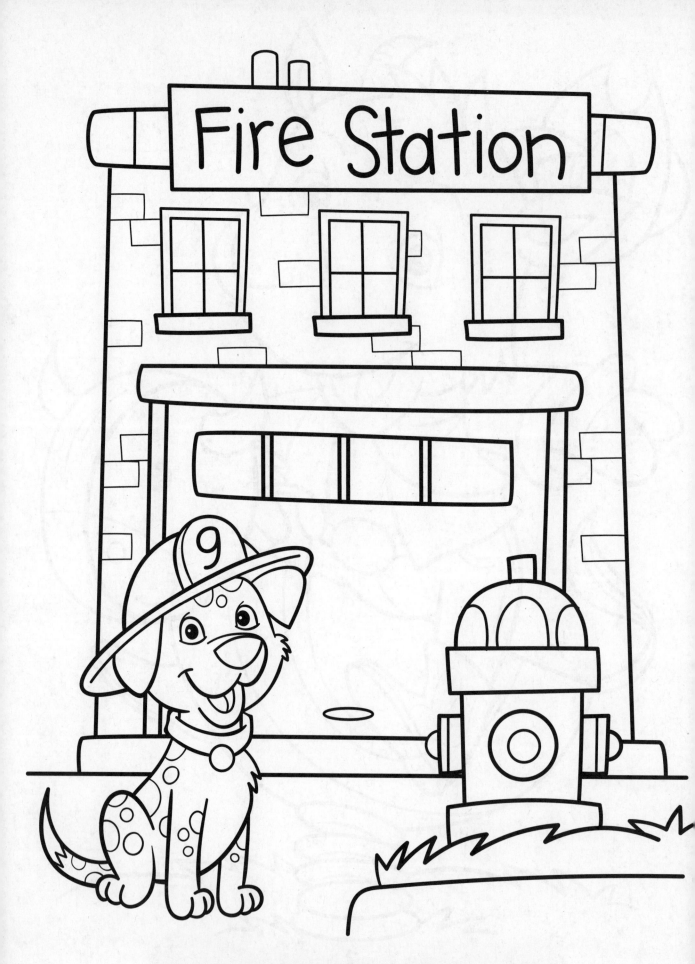

I keep guard over the fire station.

Trace over my lines so I can fly.

Crab cake, anyone?

Welcome to the pumpkin patch.

I love to visit the garden.

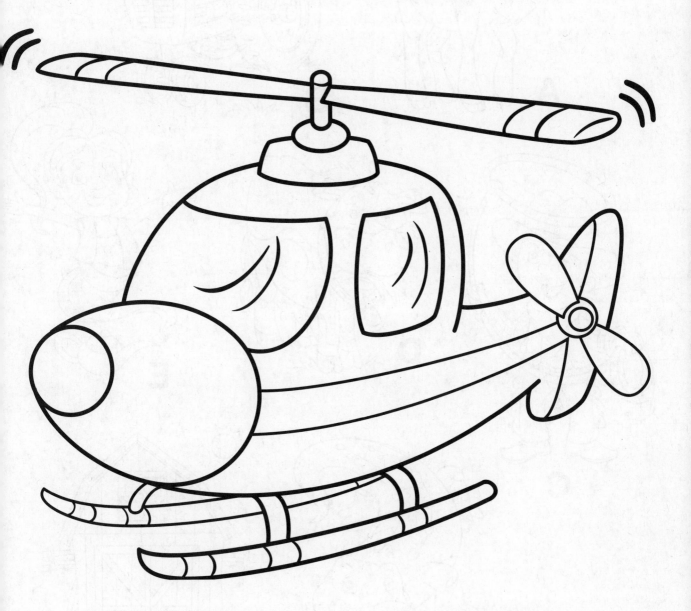

Want to take a ride in a helicopter?

A

B

C

D

E

F

G

Circle or color the things that you would see at the farm.

Chugging along, moving along.

A platypus floats through the water.

How many butterflies are in the garden?

Your answer:

Your trip can really take off at the airport.

A

B

C
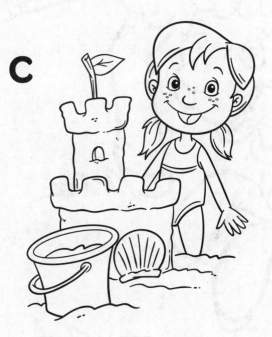

D

Your answer:

Who is exploring a different place from everyone else?

If you wander off, I'll hear your bell.

**Trace the lines to see
who is looking at you at the zoo.**

Winnings from games at a roadside fair.

A

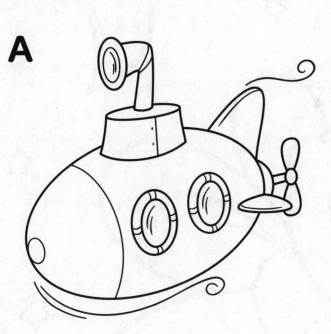

B

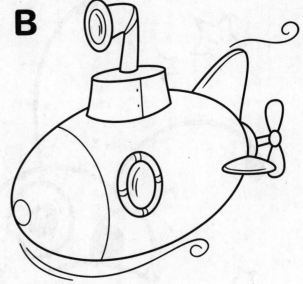

C

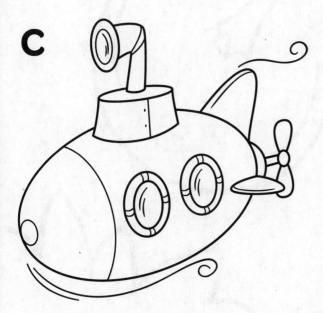

D

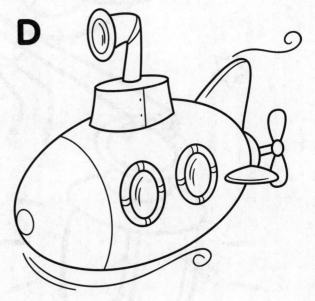

Which submarine is different?

Let me light your way.

You never know who you'll meet in the ocean.

A

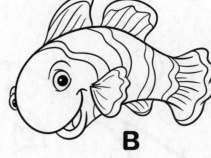

B

C

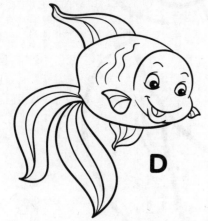

D

E

F

G

H

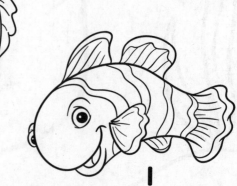

I

Find the aquarium fish that isn't part of a pair.

It's good luck to spot a ladybug.

Greetings from

Draw the thing you liked best from your last road trip and address this postcard to your best friend. Show it to them next time you see each other.

PLACE
STAMP
HERE

_____
_____
_____
_____

It's good luck to spot a ladybug

Snuggling keeps penguins warm in the cold.

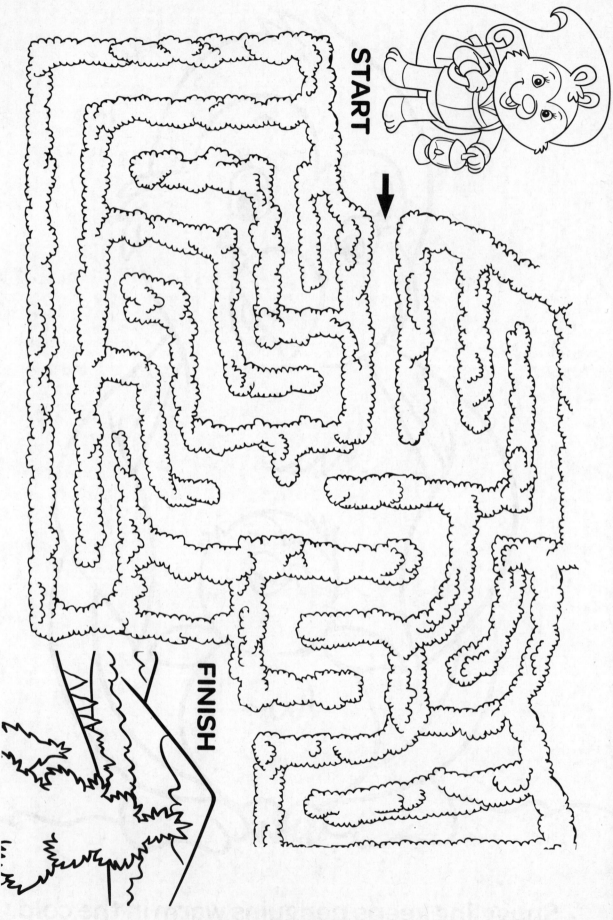

START

FINISH

Get this camper to the mountain.

Ready to sightsee from the river?

Would you swim a mile for that smile?

**Circle your favorite dino
at the museum, then color them all.**

I'm just strolling through the grass.

Check out my antlers!

A

B

C

D

E

F

Circle, then color the things that start with the letter W.

Let's set sail.

Want to play hide-and-seek?

I can't fly, but you should see me run!

My job is to keep the farm crops safe from birds. How am I doing?

How many birds do you see?

Your answer:

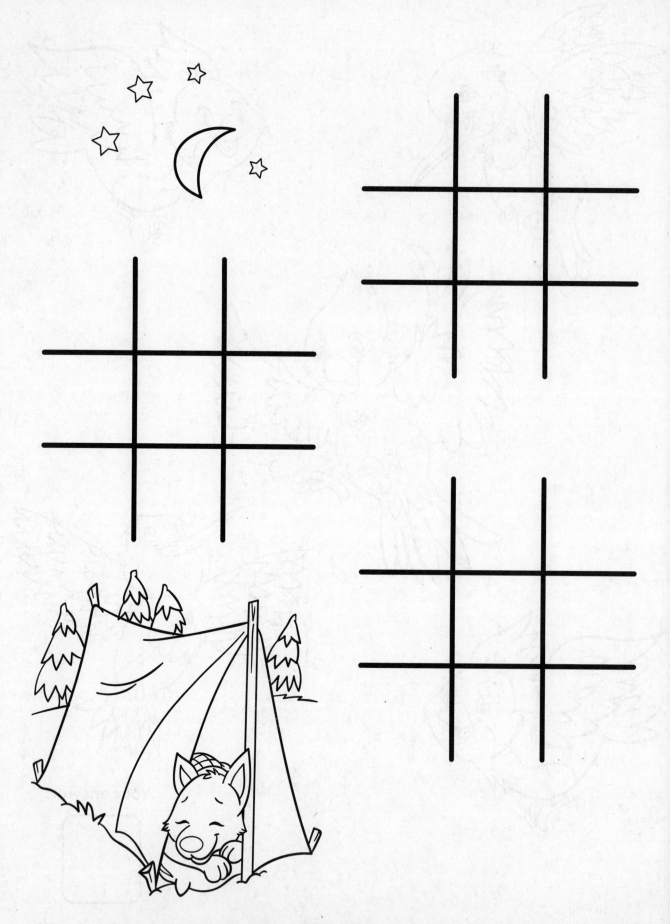

How about some tic-tac-toe before you turn in?

Just call me the King of the Sea.

I'll hold my tail. You hold your nose.

START

FINISH

Which way to the airport?

I'm just hanging out at the zoo.

Circle your favorite special treat,
then color them all.

Don't miss this cute tiger cub at the zoo.

How many of each shell
did you find at the beach?

Howdy! How was your day on the road?

Join me on a turkey trot around the farm.

Two more cookies for the road, please.

**Slow and steady, it's
the only way to travel.**

Make way for the police car.

START

FINISH

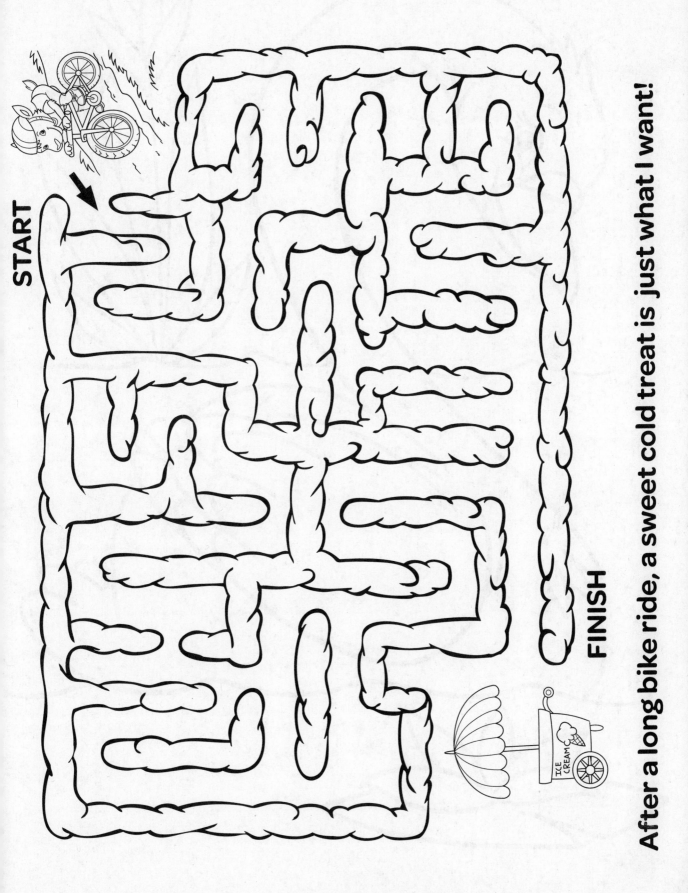

After a long bike ride, a sweet cold treat is just what I want!

Want to paddle around the pond with me?

I'm the King of the Jungle—and of the zoo, too.

Who do you think is behind the barn door?

I'm off to explore the woods. Want to come?

Make a postcard for your favorite animal at the zoo. Draw something you think he would like.

PLACE
STAMP
HERE

_____

_____

_____

_____

I'm ready to get to work and
help build a new road.

Lots of people try to see me every year, but I hide in this lake.

Make a wish.

Choo Choo! This train is ready to roll.

I love camping under the stars. . . . Zzzzz.

Trace this rabbit. Don't forget the tail!

It looks like a beautiful day for a walk.

I've got my own little mountain.

I'm very popular at the zoo—come see me!

A

B

C

D

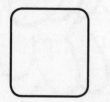

Your answer:

Which treehouse is different?

Let's share some tasty flowers.

I slither my way through the water.

This dinosaur exhibit looks so real.

This bus is waiting to take you anywhere you want to go.

When I come in for a landing, let's play some tic-tac-toe.

Next stop, Earth!

A

B

C

D

Your answer:

Which hayride is different from the rest?

This puffin keeps her eyes on the ocean.

Travel without a care, high in the air.

Fishing can be so peaceful.

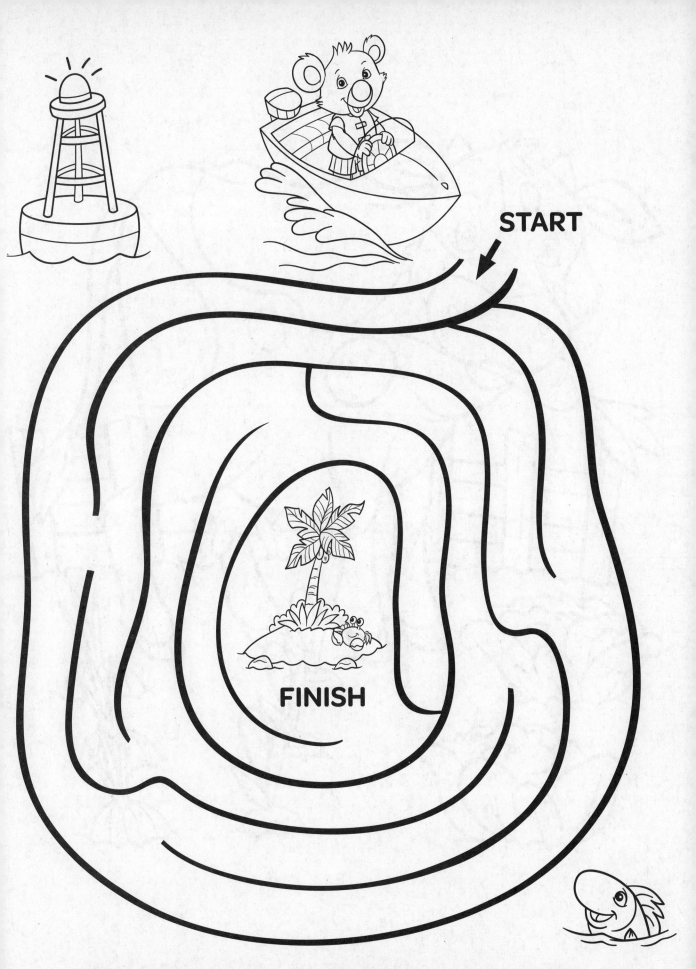

START

FINISH

Get the koala to his buddy on the island.

Did you think only rabbits like carrots?

Ah, that's the spot.

One scoop or two?

We always take the long way,
so we don't miss a thing.

**Connect the dots to see
someone spotted at the zoo.**

It's always time for a bear hug.

I traveled all over the park
to get all these acorns!

START

See how quickly you can reach the finish line.

Son, you quack me up.

Welcome to my tree.

Who do you think lives here?

Would you like to explore another planet?

I'm all packed. Now, where should I go?

Look who's smiling at the aquarium.

I'll race anyone who's willing!

Good morning from the farm.

Bring this dinosaur to life by giving her bright colors.

**Circle the vehicle you'd most like
to ride in. Then, color them all.**

I just flew in this morning.

Connect the dots to see someone who lives on land and in the water.

Greetings from

PLACE STAMP HERE

Draw a place you'd like to visit, and address this postcard to yourself!

What colors should this fire truck be?

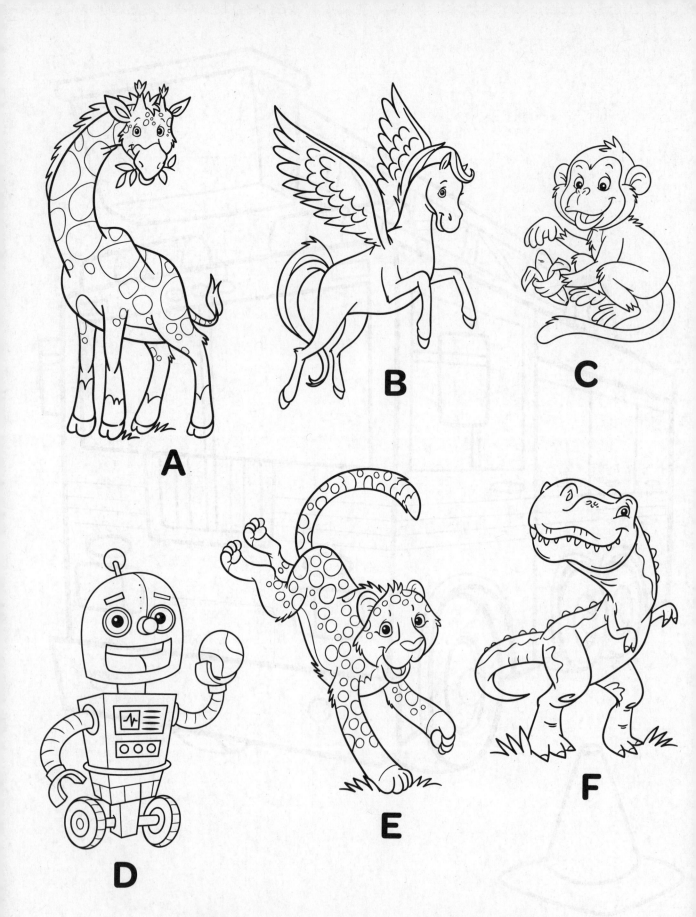

A

B

C

D

E

F

Circle, then color the animals
that you would see at the zoo.

Your cat may not like to take this trip,
but it's important she visits
the vet for a checkup.

This looks like a lovely vacation spot.

START

FINISH

HOME

Exploring is fun, but it's time to go home.

Take me for a ride around the farm?

**No matter where you are,
there's always something new to see.**

A   B   C

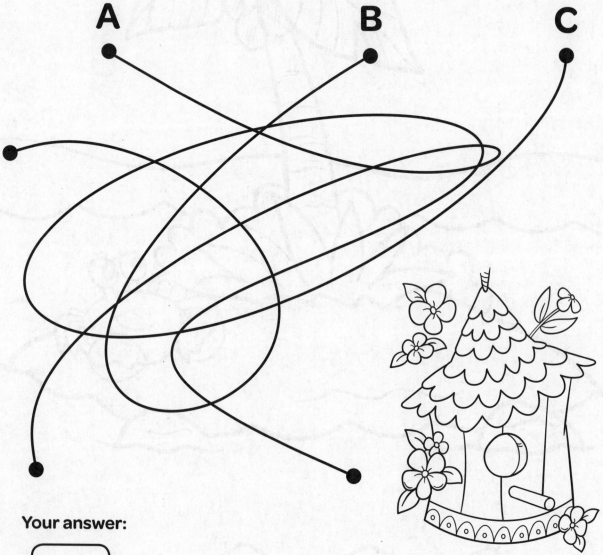

Your answer:

Which path will get the bird back home?

There's no need to stay indoors on a rainy day.
Go make a splash!

I feel so light in the water.

I just flew in to check on my eggs.

I bake roaring good cupcakes.

**This is one way to travel
by car and boat.**

How nice of the farmer to gather
all these carrots just for me.

After my bowl of milk,
I'll be ready for a catnap.

I've got to keep my teeth white
so I can flash a dazzling
smile to aquarium visitors.

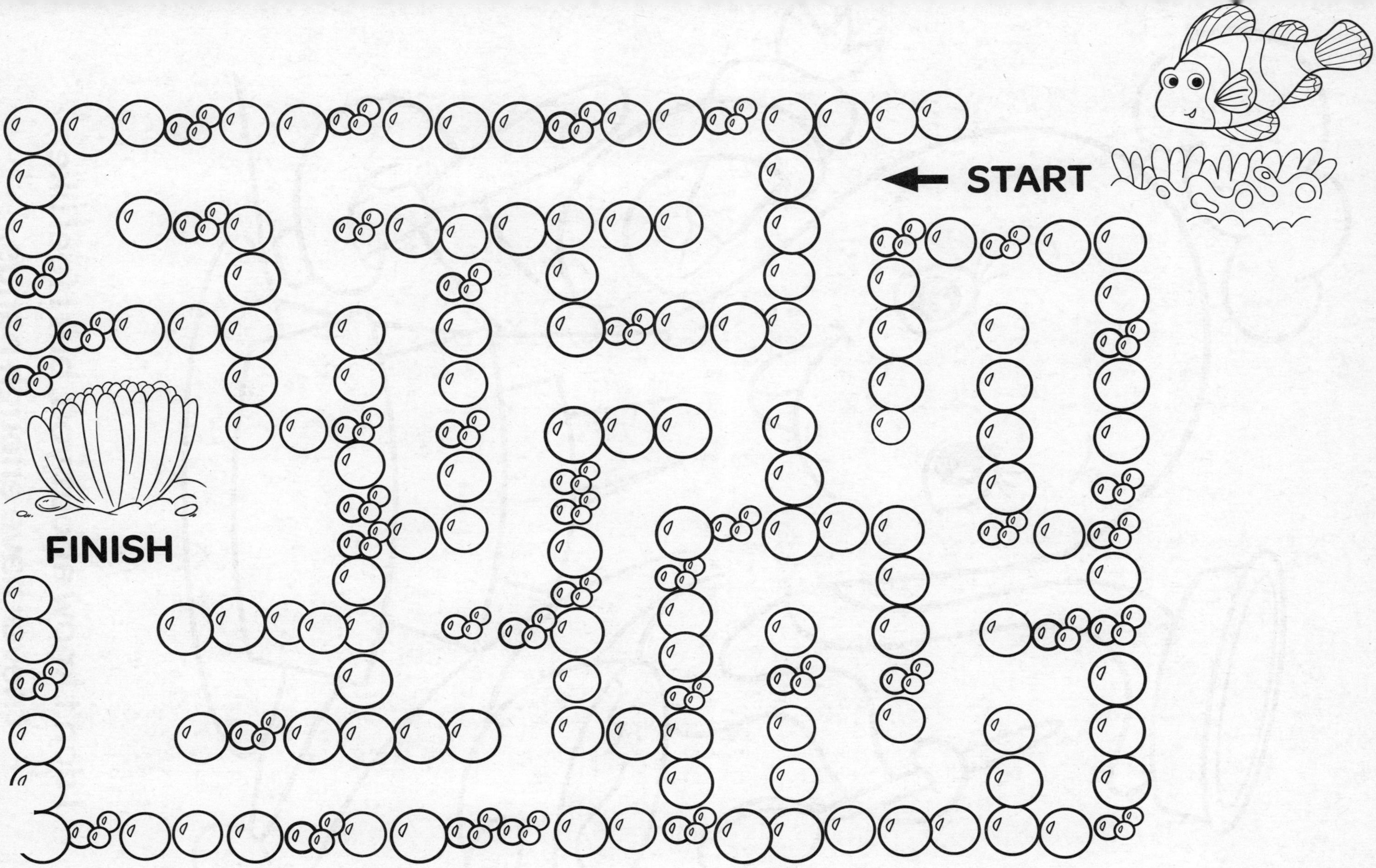

START

FINISH

Help me swim to my anemone home.

I don't know about you, but I feel like
I never have enough hands.

We're headed for adventure.

A

B

C

D

E

Circle, then color the things that start with the letter A.

Wow, this aquarium makes me feel like I'm in the water!

Want to take a hike in the mountains?

Skating in the park.

There's nothing like the great outdoors.

This is the place for stargazing.

Snowboarding is where it's at.

It's time for a dip in the pool.

How about a ski vacation?

**Finish the drawing of this rocket
so it can blast off.**

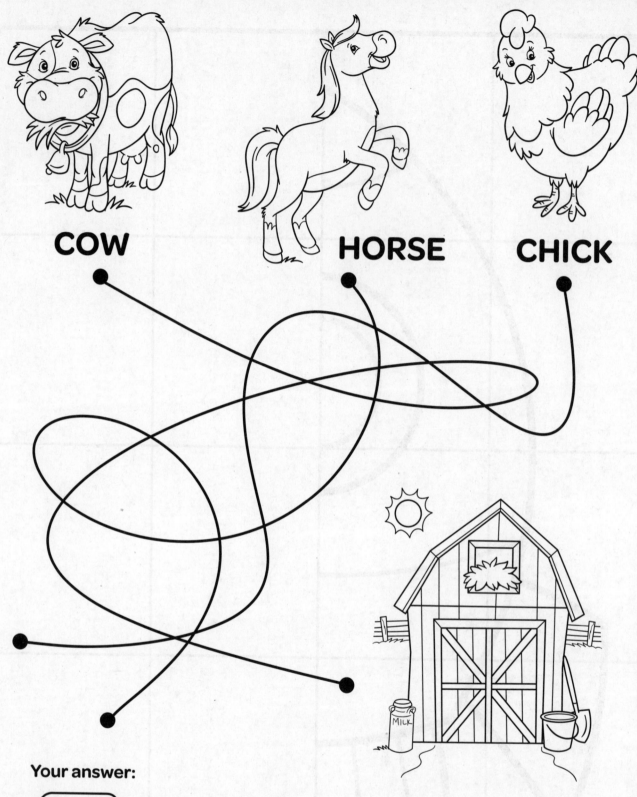

COW

HORSE

CHICK

Your answer:

Who on the farm wants
to get to the barn?

Heading to the river for some fun.

I saw you arrive at the zoo today.
Thanks for visiting.